This
Treasure Cove Story
belongs to

_____

ALL-STAR PUPS!

A CENTUM BOOK 978-1-912396-24-5
Published in Great Britain by Centum Books Ltd.
This edition published 2018. 1 3 5 7 9 10 8 6 4 2

Centum Books Ltd, 20 Devon Square, Newton Abbot,
Devon, TQ12 2HR, UK.

www.centumbooksltd.co.uk | books@centumbooksltd.co.uk
CENTUM BOOKS Limited Reg.No. 07641486.

A CIP catalogue record for this book is available
from the British Library.

Printed in China.

centum

nickelodeon

A Treasure Cove Story

ALL-STAR PUPS!

Adapted by Mary Tillworth • Illustrated by Fabrizio Petrossi
Based on the teleplay 'The Pups Save a Basketball Game' by Kim Duran

One morning, the PAW Patrol pups were playing basketball with Mayor Goodway. Skye made a Super Skye Hook right into the hoop! Rocky did his Rocky Spin and Shoot – *swish!* Then it was Marshall's turn.

'Here comes my famous Dalmatian Dunk!' he said, jumping high in the air. But he missed the hoop and bounced right into Foggy Bottom's Mayor Humdinger.

'If you blundering beagles need lessons,' grumbled Mayor Humdinger, 'my undefeated Foggy Bottom basketball team would be happy to help.'

Mayor Goodway folded her arms. 'Bring on your Boomers, Mayor. Tomorrow you'll see that Adventure Bay has the top team!'

But Mayor Goodway had forgotten one thing: Adventure Bay didn't have a basketball team. She immediately called Ryder.

'No job is too big, no pup is too small – for basketball!' Ryder declared. 'PAW Patrol, to the Lookout!'

'We only have one day to get ready,' Ryder told the pups at the Lookout. 'Chase, I'll need you to use your whistle, megaphone and traffic cones to help run the practice. Marshall, I'll need you standing by with water and ice to make sure no one gets overheated. The rest of you pups – I need you to be the team!'

Later, at the basketball court, Chase set up a running-and-bouncing drill.

'Okay, team, let's see some hustle!' he said.

As Marshall dribbled the basketball, it bounced out of control and he tripped over the cones.

The pups piled into a pyramid next
to the hoop. Marshall tried to pass the
ball and took a tumble instead! Luckily,
Skye nudged the ball into the hoop
at the last second.

On the big day, the mayor gave Ryder and the pups a team name: the Adventure Bay All-Stars! But they didn't feel like all-stars. They felt nervous, especially Marshall.

'I don't think I should play in the game,' he said to Ryder. 'If someone gets hurt, I want to be ready.'

'Are you sure that's the reason?' asked Ryder.

Marshall nodded, but he was secretly worried that he wasn't good enough to be on the team.

The Adventure Bay All-Stars lined up against the Foggy Bottom Boomers. Rubble and a Boomer faced off at the centre. Cap'n Turbot was the referee.

'Okay, players. Let's see super sportsmanship for this sporting spectacle!' He tossed the basketball into the air and the game was on!

The Boomer leapt up and
knocked the ball away from Rubble.
Foggy Bottom had the advantage!

The ball bounced to a Boomer, who took
a shot – and scored!
'Just let us know when you've had enough,
Mayor Goodway!' chuckled Mayor Humdinger.

At the end of the court, Ryder passed the ball to Rocky. The pup dribbled down the court, dodging Boomers left and right!

Rocky threw the ball to Skye, who flipped it towards the hoop. The Adventure Bay All-Stars and the Foggy Bottom Boomers were tied, 2-2!

The Boomers headed down the court and then, suddenly, Zuma stole the ball and passed it to Ryder. Ryder dribbled, weaved past a Boomer, shot and scored!

Up and down the court the players dribbled, shot and scored... and the Adventure Bay All-Stars were winning!

'I can't believe the pups are ahead... I mean, go, All-Stars!' cheered Mayor Goodway.

Mayor Humdinger twirled his moustache and whispered to a Boomer, 'You know what to do.'

As Rocky and Zuma headed
down the court, a Boomer stuck
out his foot and sent them tumbling!

From the sidelines, Marshall raced to the rescue. He bandaged Rocky's sprained paw and put an ice pack on Zuma's tail to keep the swelling down.

'Do you want to play?' Ryder asked Marshall. 'We need you. Otherwise, we don't have enough players.'

Marshall hung his head. 'I'm kind of clumsy with the ball.'

'It doesn't matter how good you are – you're a part of our team!' said Chase. 'Come on! No game is too big, no pup is too small!'

With Marshall on the team, the All-Stars trotted onto the court. When Ryder missed a foul shot, Marshall dived for the rebound, but a Boomer beat him to it.

Ryder patted Marshall. 'Don't worry. You'll get it next time.'

As the clock ticked down to the final seconds, the All-Stars were losing, 43-42.

'Marshall!' called Ryder as he passed the ball to him.

'*Whoaaa!*' Marshall landed on top of the ball and rolled right past the Boomer defence.

Marshall was still struggling to control the ball. He dived on top of it and both the ball and the pup bounced high in the air and right into the hoop!

The final buzzer sounded. On the scoreboard, the All-Stars had 44 points and the Boomers had 43. Marshall had scored the winning basket for the Adventure Bay All-Stars!

Ryder reached up to help Marshall
down. 'Great move, Marshall!'
'You won the game!' cheered Skye.
Ryder smiled. 'If you ever need some
all-star players, just yelp for help!'

 # Treasure Cove Stories

An ongoing series to collect and enjoy!